War: The Diary of the Alpha Female

Gloria Sicilia Bellator Gabrei

outskirtspress
DENVER, COLORADO

War: The Diary of the Alpha Female
All Rights Reserved.
Copyright © 2015 Gloria Sicilia Bellator Gabrei
v2.0

Outskirts Press, Inc.
http://www.outskirtspress.com

ISBN: 978-1-4787-3958-6

Outskirts Press and the "OP" logo are trademarks belonging to Outskirts Press, Inc.

PRINTED IN THE UNITED STATES OF AMERICA

FRIDAY MARCH 13, 2020

MY MOTHER FOUND an empty book and told me to start writing my story. She always told me, "No one's story is the same. Even if it's the same event, the stories are always different because of point of view." My mother was a large Great Dane with a black stripe that goes from the nape of her neck straight to the tip of her nose. She had warm brown eyes that sparkled with kindness and were filled with motherly love. Her name was Roga.

She often spoke of my father; he was the Alpha Male of a pack of wolves. My father was a red wolf with black stripes that reminded me of the stripes on a tiger's pelt. His name was Achilles because he was the greatest fighter in the forest.

I lived with my mother in town instead of with my father because my father had a whole pack to keep him from being alone, but my mother had only me. My mother also told me that I had six older half-brothers from my father's first mate. She told me their names were Luka, Tiberius,

Spartacus, Odysseus, Brutus, and Ajax. Their mother died somehow and then our father met my mother and they had me.

My mother also told stories of how the humans had managed to successfully teach a few animals how to write and speak the human language. When the animals discovered this they began teaching their family and friends how to speak and write; until this new knowledge was taught to every animal. That was five years ago, long before both of us were born.

She always found some time in her stories to mention the psychic gifts that God gives each animal, and that night was one of those times. "Mysty, I have to talk to you about tomorrow night." My mother sounded somber so I knew something was wrong.

"Yes Mama. What is it?"

"In my dream, God sent me a message of the future; all animals were at war with humans."

"All?! But, that makes no sense; animals have never organized a war against the humans!"

"I know that Sweetie, but that is what I saw and my visions have never been wrong."

"Who won?" I had to ask even though I knew what she was going to say.

"You know I can't see that far, and besides, God wouldn't have revealed that to me anyway. He knows who is going to win and that is all that matters."

"When will it happen?"

"I don't know, but the fight I was watching looked like it was taking place in the present, so I'm sending you to live with your father so he can train you to fight."

"Will you come too Mama?"

"No Sweetie, my place is here, I am not meant to live in the wild."

"I'll see you again though, won't I?"

"Eventually, but until then, I think you'll enjoy the wild more than the town."

I knew that my mother was right, I always had hated living in this terrible, dirty little town, maybe a change of scenery was exactly what I needed.

SUNDAY MARCH 15, 2020

MY MOTHER DIED last night. She was gathering food from the dumpster, when she was discovered by a few teenage humans with guns. They shot her down in cold blood, but she didn't die instantly. She tried to crawl back to our alley, but the leader of the group shot her in the head and she died after that. I couldn't believe that someone as kind hearted and loving as my mother could just be shot down as if she was a can of beer that they were using for target practice.

I knew that I should have felt remorse, but instead I felt fury dwelling inside me. They had no right to take the innocent life of a mother dog just because they felt it would humor them. As I watched them walk away, they were laughing about my mother's death and bragging at their good aiming skills. I looked back down at my mother's lifeless body, her blood was pooling the edge of the alley and her body was mangled by the bullets. She did not deserve to die like that!

I tried to control my rage, but it spilled out of me and I ran after those humans. I hunted down all three of them and I attacked them. I ripped into their pelts and I snapped their bones with my powerful wolf jaws. I did look like a wolf, but I was as tall as a Great Dane, I was easily able to overpower the teenage humans. After mauling them, I left them there to either die from blood loss or be saved by their fellow humans. I had just shown my mother's killers the mercy they never gave her.

I went back to the alley and buried my mother's body in the dirt of the alley, that's where she belonged. At midnight, my father came to my alley and I told him about what happened to his mate. I told him about my retaliation too just in case he discovered any human bodies on his way over here. I knew that because he too had done the same thing once, he would at least understand my motif if not approve of it.

"I know that was a terrible way for you to lose your mother, but violence must only be your last resort. Those humans had guns on them and as you have witnessed by your mother's tragic death, they knew how to use them and they would not have hesitated. Besides, God doesn't like revenge."

"Yeah, I guess so, but I couldn't control myself no matter how hard I tried."

"It happens to all of us Mysty," my father tried to comfort me, but I was inconsolable, "be brave my daughter.

You are a warrior now." He looked down at his paws; he was grieving for her too.

It was then that I noticed my father had opposable thumbs! In shock I gasped and asked, "Daddy, where did those come from?"

"We've been taking the humans' technology and making use of it, just like your thumbs, when you were just a week old, I put those thumbs on you so you could write. All animals used to have them until the humans stole them, so we took them back." My father proudly announced, "Well, I say we should leave now, we want to be back before dawn or my pack will start to worry."

I too wanted to leave that place behind as swiftly as possible. I didn't want to stay there any longer because the memory of my mother's horrific death was too painful to enable me to stay, and I was excited a little because I wanted to meet my half-brothers, I had never had a sibling before so I looked at it as a wonderful opportunity to see what it was like not only having siblings, but also being the youngest.

MONDAY MARCH 16, 2020

I MET MY brothers and I like them. Luka was the oldest so I wanted to meet him first. He looked just like Achilles except Luka had more stripes than our father. Their eyes were the same color too, amber. Tiberius and Spartacus were twins, but Tiberius was born first so I met Tiberius and then Spartacus. Tiberius had his mother's white fur and our father's black stripes, he also had amber eyes. Spartacus had the exact opposite fur as his twin. Spartacus had black fur with white stripes, and his mother's forest green eyes. Odysseus is the oddest looking of the bunch, he had brown fur with the same black patch pattern of a Rottweiler, but his eyes were the same color as our father's eyes. Brutus had a snow white pelt and eyes so forest green that they were almost black. Ajax was the youngest so he was the last brother I was introduced to. Ajax had red fur and light forest green eyes.

Then I saw a giant dog that appeared to be a cross between a Mastiff and a German Shepherd. As he got closer, I could tell that he is about two months older than me. I also saw his interesting German Shepherd patches, his patches were multicolored they were dark brown, dark tan, and dark fawn. The rest of his pelt was a night black color. He walked up to where we were and asked, "Who's the wolf dog?"

"My other sister Mysty," Brutus said with a hint of annoyance.

"Other?!" I gasped.

"Yeah, don't you remember Missi, your older twin?" Brutus was confused at how shocked I was to hear that I had a twin.

"I don't think Roga told her." My father mumbled as he appeared behind us.

"Hello, Achilles." The German Shepard mutt greeted by dipping his head in respect.

"I see that you have taken an interest in my daughter." Achilles pointed out, "And I would prefer that Eudorus not know that she is my daughter. You know how he is."

"That won't be a problem." The dog assured him.

"Go on back to the patrol, Flippy; we need to make sure we have all the help we can get from our neighboring packs."

Flippy gave my father a puppyish smile and left the clearing. I think I have a crush.

THURSDAY MARCH 19, 2020

I HAD BEEN very busy training, but I had still been able to notice Flippy's absence. I couldn't get him off my mind, he was such a sweet dog and he acted very puppyish, but I could tell that he was a very skilled fighter. I knew that it's only been a few days but it seemed like years. I did the best I could to block Flippy from my mind but, I had barely managed to keep my crush on Flippy a secret from my family, just as my family was trying hard to keep my birth parents a secret from the rest of the pack. Only my family and Flippy knew about my secret identity.

Since Luka is the oldest and the second – in – command, he took it upon himself to introduce me to the rest of the pack. As far as they knew, I was just a wolf dog who may be interested in helping a wolf pack fight a war against humans (with the help other animals, of course).

Today Luka told me the names of some of our pack members, "The pack isn't as big as it once was because of the patrols. But at the time we have Tyler and his brother

Trevor, then over there is Rose talking to a few of the elderly wolves, Crispin, Triopas, and Nestor, although none are as old as Eudorus, who is sitting right over there by the tree. And over there by the hill is Hector and his friend Paris, just under the hill is Hector's sister, Helen and Paris's sister Pandora. Over by the creek are Pisces and his little sisters Siri and Tea. Then we have Ticeson and his cousin Velior. That's Aeneas over by the ditch and his sisters Andromache and Briseis, also over there is Thistle and his twin sister Thorn who's playing with Heather. Slash and Fang are standing by those bushes they're sisters. And then we have Iron and his friend Titan over by Eudorus."

"Why can't Eudorus know who I am?" I asked Luka curiously.

"Eudorus is the oldest wolf any of us have ever known so we respect him, and because he's an Old One he is the advisor of the Alpha. His youngest daughter was my mother, and when she died, he became obsessed with Alpha Females not being allowed to fight, because there is a chance that both Alphas could die and if they didn't appoint a second – in – command then that leaves the pack vulnerable."

"So if he knew that I was a candidate for the role of Alpha Female then he wouldn't let me fight?"

"Mysty, if our father were to die, you would be the Alpha Female until I found a mate."

"But what about Tiberius, or Spartacus, or Odysseus, or Brutus, or even Ajax?"

"They were not appointed second – in – command so unless I appointed one of them before I died; you would be the only Alpha. Oh, and I think you should keep your distance from Eudorus too."

"Why? If no one has told him about me then we should have nothing to worry about, and he can't see my Alpha gem." The Alpha gem was a leather strap that held one gem, that one gem was to show other animals that you were the sibling, mate, or offspring of an Alpha.

"That may be true, but you look just like Missi, and if Eudorus studies you long enough he may be able to put two and two together. Where did you hide the gem?"

"My fur is thick enough, no one has been able to see it so far, just as long as I keep my fur down and a breeze doesn't catch me by surprise."

"How long have you had it?" Luka questioned.

"Since I was a week old, now will someone please tell me about my sister?" I whined in frustration.

"Alright, alright. When you two were a month old, our father wanted to train at least one of you to be a fight-er. Roga gave him Missi since she was the eldest and you were a runt. After just a month of training, she managed to defeat me in battle, she was very skilled and everyone in the pack loved her. Then one day, a trespassing human dog-napped her. No one has seen her since."

As I listened to the story of my older sister's disappearance, my mind drifted back to Flippy, "Why is Flippy named that?"

"Flippy got his name because when he was three weeks old, he actually did a perfect back flip. His parents were escaped pets and they thought that what their son was doing was a disgrace because their humans used to force them to do back flips. So they named him Flippy to remind him to never again do a back flip. They died a few months ago and once our father found out Flippy could do back flips like our pack members, he insisted that Flippy use his back flip skills in battle."

I took this information and thought about how that must have been for him. My thoughts however, were quickly interrupted by my father; he decided to call a pack meeting now that the messenger birds had informed him of who would help in the fight.

"I'm afraid that our help has been greatly decreased as the humans are progressing through the forest. Our patrols are returning and once they do, I am breaking every one into teams of two. Right now, I shall inform you of your partner so that when the patrol returns, you will know who your partner is."

I was so happy to know that my war partner was going to be Flippy! I couldn't believe my luck!

WEDNESDAY APRIL 1, 2020

FLIPPY RETURNED TODAY! Once I told him we were going to be partners he seemed very happy about it too. Scamandrius reported to my father, when his patrol returned, about the humans who were closing in on the pack's location. My father decided that we should retreat to the "Safe City" as it was called.

I figured I should ask Flippy about the Safe City and he told me, "The Safe City was built by some humans that believed in the preservation of wild animals. The city has very tall walls that stretch up to a hundred feet. Once it came to building the actual city however, they ran out of metal and the spacious apartments were made out of a special wood that never rots. We have never used it before but I think now would be a good time to do just that."

"Wouldn't they be able to fly over us and bomb the city?" I questioned.

"No, our city poses an emergency roof, and besides that, humans stopped making planes."

Just then my father decided to announce who was assigned which weapons before we arrived at the Safe City. "The humans who worked in creating the weapons have rebelled against their Alphas for not giving them what they want, so our weapons and theirs have become more primitive. You have all been taught hand to paw combat, so now you must learn how to use a weapon, based on your strengths; I have assigned you all weapons.

I noticed that while everyone else seemed to know what to do with theirs, I did not. I just knew about hand to paw combat, and I was so good at it that I had managed to beat all of my brothers except for Luka and so I still didn't have a chance against my father. I may have had opposable thumbs ever since my first week but that didn't mean I was a professional at shooting a bow and arrow. Luckily my father saw my helplessness and started training me how to shoot. I surprised myself by hitting the target almost every time. I was enjoying myself for once since my mother died.

My father had told me we will be moving into the city tomorrow.

THURSDAY APRIL 2, 2020

AS WE WERE leaving, Tod volunteered to stay behind to tell the other animals that the wolves were awaiting them at the Safe City. When we arrived at the city's walls I was in complete awe. I couldn't believe how big the Safe City was. My father showed us where the secret hatch was located and I was surprised to find that it was just two simple cellar doors that were made out of wood instead of metal.

"Why aren't these doors made out of metal too?" I asked my father.

"There's no need Sweet One, the doors lead into many booby trapped passage ways. Only those who have been in the city before know the true secret passage way into the city. Even if the humans had one of their pets help them sniff out our trail, the pet would instantly become confused since everyday someone lays down scent markers to prevent the humans' slaves from entering." He answered.

Once we entered the city, I saw a building that was taller than all the others around it. My father saw me gazing at it and grinned before he said, "Now normally only the Alphas and their family members get to be in this building, but since you are one of the best fighters in this pack, I'm making you the pack army's second – in – command. The leader of the pack army is Luka."

"So I get to sleep in this building?" I asked my father hoping that he would allow me to since we were pretending I wasn't his kin.

"Go on in and pick your room, and if I were you, I'd pick the room at the top. It has a better view of the landscape and an access to the roof." My father whispered.

I glanced at my father with a puzzled look, but he didn't seem to notice and he moved on with the rest of the group, leaving me and my brothers alone.

"I've been here before Mysty, once we pick out our rooms, I'll lead the rest of the tour until we catch up to them." Luka said to me as if he could read my mind. Then again, for all I knew, he could.

I did as my father suggested and picked the top room, and he was right. I did have a perfect view of the battle field! But my favorite part (aside from the roof access) was the balcony. From the balcony, I could see the battle field from the comfort of a soft rug. And I also loved my fluffy dog bed that felt like a cloud.

Once I was finished touring my room, I met my

brothers outside and Luka showed us the rest of the city, including the Meeting Hall, where Alphas and their advisors discussed pressing issues, then there was the Clinic Building, where all the sick and injured were cared for, and then we met back up with our father at the Meal Hall.

"Ah! There you are, I was wondering when you would catch up." He greeted us.

"It wouldn't have been such a long wait if Ajax would learn how to make up his mind." Luka grumbled as he glared at Ajax making him lower his head in guilt. I then realized that no matter how hard any of us tried, Luka would always be deadly serious.

"Well now that you are all settled, I think it's time for our meal." My father quickly changed the subject.

"What are we having? Is it elk? Is it deer? Or is it prairie chicken?! I hope it's prairie chicken!" I barked in anticipation.

"Sorry to disappoint you Sweet One, but out of respect for our allies some of which happen to be those animals you just listed, we'll be eating a different kind of meat, one that you've never had before."

"Really? What would that be?"

"Let's just say that unlike the humans, we don't waste what we kill." My father gave me a sly smile while I remained confused.

Once we entered the huge Meal Hall, I saw a long

table in the middle and other slightly shorter tables. "This table in the center is for Alphas, their kin, the advisors, and the leaders of the armies." Achilles explained to me.

"Will I be eating here too?" I wasn't sure since no one was supposed to know that I was his daughter.

"Yes. Don't worry about Eudorus; he'll just think that you are an important member of the army, like maybe, the army's leader?"

"What are you saying? You want me to be the army's leader?"

"That is Luka's job; yours will be as his second – in – command. If anything happens to him, you will take his place. Now then, time for us to take our seats."

I sat towards the middle of the table's left side, and I waited to see what we would be eating. Soon, an elk entered the room, with a large platter on his head resting in between his antlers; he set it down it at the front end of the table and quickly left the room. Another elk did the same to the other tables.

"Why did they just do that?" I asked Flippy.

"The elk are thankful that we showed them the city because it is a haven to them, a place where they don't have to live in fear, and in their gratitude, they have offered to serve us our meals."

As the mystery meat made its way down the table I realized that it smelt familiar. Once I took my share off of the platter and placed it onto my area of the table I realized what it was instantly. "This was a human!" I gasped quietly.

"Yep, what we kill we eat, we do not take pictures of our prey, or chop off pieces of the carcass and waste the rest, nor do we have our prey stuffed. We only kill what we have to in order to survive." Flippy whispered.

"I possibly killed and it wasn't for food." I mumbled as I poked at the hunk of human flesh, no longer feeling hungry.

"We've all done things we aren't proud of, Mysty. I too have killed once for revenge and I've regretted it ever since because I realized that by doing so, I was no better than them. But then Achilles showed me that even though I did that, I was not in my right mind and therefore, it could be forgiven since it was my first time, but if I ever did it again, only then could it be counted against me."

"What about this war?" I asked him.

"What do you think we are going to be eating while we're stuck in the city? Once we fight the humans off the battle field, the elk will help us carry their dead in the city while their injured are left on the battle field until they are dead or retrieved by their comrades."

"That's interesting." I decided as I began biting into the flesh of the human. "Wow! This is delicious!"

"I thought so too the first time I had a bite." Flippy agreed.

"I wonder why I didn't eat human before." I joked.

"You're not the only one."

After our meal we all went to our rooms for the night.

FRIDAY APRIL 3, 2020

TODAY THE WAR began.

Tod never made it back to the city, he was the first to be killed as he lead the persecuting humans away from the rest of our animal army who were just making their way into the city. I felt very sorry for Tod and his partner Tabitha.

"Alright," my father began to dish out orders, "Every one whose weapons are swords, knives, and Tasers are to fight outside. You must stay near the city's walls in case we need to make a swift retreat. All healers or any one whose weapons are arrows, guns, or bombs are to stay inside until the battle is over."

He began stationing the bombers, archers, and gunners around the ledges at the top of the city's walls, "I want two bombers in the front, and two stationed on the right and left sides. I want two gunners in the front corners of the left and right walls. As for the archers, I want four on each side of the walls, including the back just in case the humans want to try something creative. Mysty, I want you to climb on top of that pole and tell me when the humans arrive."

"And when they do?" I wondered what I should do next.

"After the humans arrive join the archers at the front wall." my father decided.

I obeyed my father and kept a look out for the humans. My father didn't fight today since he had to wait to meet with the other Alphas before he could enter combat (much to his annoyance). The other Alphas gave the same grouping orders to their warriors while I waited to give them the warning signal.

I didn't have too long to wait before the humans started to appear on the horizon. Which was also when I noticed they had Tod's body hanging off of a flag pole like a trophy. I quickly alerted my father and the other Alphas before joining the other archers by Flippy's side.

"They killed Tod." I sighed sadly.

"He was a fine warrior and he will be missed, but he died for a good reason. He was selfless like that." Flippy shared my sorrow.

"Why were we even paired with partners if we don't get to fight with them?"

"This placement is only temporary until their numbers have gone down. We're only fighting the poachers, hunters, and others who are against animal rights. Their numbers will dwindle before ours do." Flippy assured me.

The fight started as soon as the humans were within the range of the archers. We shot off our arrows while the bombers threw their explosives into the fight and occasionally the gunners would shoot a human down. The fight lasted all day, but it was the humans who were forced to retreat. Only when every living human had vanished did we bring in our injured. Our three healers Sherry, Cherry and Carry got to work on our pack immediately.

As I watched the chaos around me, I heard Ajax screaming for Sherry.

"Don't look." Brutus urged me, but it was too late, I had already looked over my shoulder to see Odysseus lying on the ground soaked in his own blood.

Sherry, the blue wolf with the warm blue eyes ran over to Odysseus and Ajax and began working swiftly on Odysseus, but she stopped abruptly and shook her head slowly and sadly at Ajax. Ajax let out a painful howl alerting our father to the fact that he had just lost one of his sons.

I never had a chance to really get to know Odysseus, and now I never will.

SATURDAY APRIL 4, 2020

LAST NIGHT I left the city to patrol alone for a short bit. The death of my brother still hung over me like an ill omen and I desperately tried to take my mind off of it. His death was my first experience of the horrors of war. Even though we weren't close, his death was hard to accept.

Walking through the woods was comforting, but at the same time I couldn't shake the feeling I was being watched. I ignored it and believed I was just being paranoid. I instead focused on the light of the moon and admired how it shot out rays of light through the trees much like the sun did during the early hours of morning.

I was shocked back to reality by the flapping of wing beats behind me, swiftly followed by, "According to my ability to interpret body language, you are somber about a tragedy that happened sometime this evening."

I turned to see a pair of large black eyes gazing at me through the leafy branches of a nearby tree. I studied the animal for a few seconds, her eyes were black as coals, her body covered in feathers, the feathers on her face were possibly white since they were now light blue due to the night sky, the rest of her feathers were a gold color tinted blue as well.

"You're a Barn Owl!" I realized surprised that she had been following me.

"Not just any Barn Owl." she pointed out.

"Who are you? I haven't seen you amongst the ranks of the Bird Army."

"No, you probably wouldn't have heard of me. I am not well known in these recent times. My name is Athena."

"Athena? Many animals seem to have these odd human sounding names. My family and I happen to be some of those animals. I'm Mysty."

"Would you like to come up to my nest? I maybe a Barn Owl, but this tree is my home. I do not uphold animal stereotypes."

I instantly started to like this sharp tonged, quick minded bird. She was funny and helped me take my mind off of Odysseus, so I of course accepted her invitation, "Yes I'd love to come up."

"Is it safe to assume that you can climb?" Athena questioned.

"I'm not an avid climber, but this tree seems simple enough." I was certain I could climb it, "By the way, your voice sounds funny."

"To me so does yours. My funny sounding voice is probably due to my accent. I grew up in England, but decided to migrate here for a better life. By the looks of things, this place is not much better."

"England? You flew all the way here from England?"

"No, I stowed away on a boat. They never go down to the cargo hold any more. Now are you going to climb up here or are you going to stay down there all night?"

I was about to climb up the tree until I heard my father's familiar howl calling for me to return. I turned back to Athena and embarrassingly asked for a rain check.

"Well you know where to find me." Athena shrugged as she entered her nest while I was forced to retreat to the city for the night.

SUNDAY APRIL 5, 2020

WE FOUGHT AGAIN today. My father reassigned partners to those who had lost theirs during the first battle.

During this battle, not many of us died, but my father was one of them. He was determined to fight in this battle, but his obsessive worry for his remaining sons had led to his downfall. This war has turned me into an orphan. It had turned my father into a Griever, but he's with Odysseus now, and my mother, and his first mate Ticura.

The day was too somber and quiet for me to want to stick around, so I left and returned to Athena's tree. She found me before I found her, "So first your brother and now your father?"

"How did you know that?"

"I have wisdom and much of it, that's why my name is Athena. Besides, word passes from ear to ear like the wind."

"Yes. I lost my brother and now I'm an orphan as well."

"Come on up Mysty, I am a healer and as such, it is my duty to heal you."

"Nothing can heal a broken heart." I reminded her as I started to climb.

"Ah, you memorized that old saying I see. But you left out that part about time."

"Time doesn't heal; it just makes the memory fuzzier as it passes."

"Losing your father and your brother is not something you can forget so easily." Athena said as she stepped back so I could squeeze into her hollowed out nest inside the tree.

"I wish I could."

"Be careful what you wish for. Irony can be a cold hearted- well that's not important." she decided.

"It must be nice to be a healer. When I was living in the city I had to memorize a few herbal remedies myself."

"Really? Are you training?"

"Oh, no. I'm a fighter and besides, I could never be as talented as the triplets."

"Sherry, Carry, and Cherry?"

"You know the triplets?" I was amazed.

"Who do you think trained them? I'm their mentor" Athena admitted proudly.

"And how did that happen?"

"Their parents were good friends of mine but they felt that their healing abilities were not as advanced as mine. They blamed it on the lack of time they spent with their mentor (while my mentor was my father). They figured that if they had a litter of pups who were raised by a proper healer, their offsprings' talents would far exceed the abilities of themselves. So they had the triplets and once the pups were weaned they were given to me to raise."

"What happened to their parents?" I asked interested by Athena's story.

"Sadly, they died six months later. Humans are so cruel, but they are also very confused. They don't have a strong belief in God. Some humans do, but most are of different faiths and some refuse to acknowledge God at all. It's so tragic."

I silently agreed with Athena; however I figured I should probably return to the city. I didn't even try to sleep that night. I was too busy questioning if we could still win the war. After all if the humans could kill my father, an undefeated warrior, was there truly any hope for us?

MONDAY APRIL 6, 2020

TODAY WAS PRETTY uneventful, but a significant event happened today any way, one I would definitely like to make note of. It was during dinner in the Meal Hall. Luka was eating with the other Alphas of the animal army, discussing something I was too far away to hear. Meanwhile, I was staring down at my empty table space. I had purposely grabbed nothing from the platter since I was not feeling hungry.

"Are you okay?" Flippy suddenly asked me.

I was instantly snapped back into reality and Flippy was sitting right next to me.

"I'm fine, thank you." I assured him, not very convincingly however.

"You haven't eaten in two days." he pointed out.

"Yes I have, you just didn't see." I defended

"No one else did either." Flippy commented dryly.

I snarled at him before I stood up and walked away from the table. My departure was of course unnoticed by all except for Flippy. I went back to my room and sat on the rug on my balcony to look out at the night sky. I soon heard a knock on my door, but I ignored it hoping that the animal would go away.

"You didn't answer so I just let myself in." Flippy said as he appeared next to me.

I still ignored him, but he refused to leave and started to talk again, "I'm worried about you."

"Why? You have no reason to be, I am fully capable of handling myself." I asserted.

"Well, I really like you and I don't want to see you get hurt."

"Too late for that now isn't it?"

"No, I meant physically. I really care about you. I was hoping you would share my feelings." Flippy had said in a rather cautious voice.

"We're partners; of course I care about you." I assured him.

I think I'm getting closer to making him my mate!

WEDNESDAY APRIL 8, 2020

WE FOUGHT AGAIN today and a lot more of us died this time. I wonder if they blame it on Luka, it was after all his first battle as an Alpha and I had not yet been awarded the position of the wolf army's leader. He does feel guilty, but maybe after such a tragic loss a thing like this was expected.

After mourning our fallen warriors, I snuck out to Athena's tree once more. I think she wanted me to be a healer and I was interested, so I wanted to learn all I could from her. Once I arrived she began talking about all these healing tips, but I must admit it was slightly boring. I decided to break away from listening to her tips by asking her, "What was your most challenging case?"

"Ah! I'd say that would be the time when a pretty white wolf with these forest green eyes, she was about five years old and she was crossing the road at night but was hit by a car. It was a hit and run. Luckily I was there, but she had multiple broken bones and internal bleeding.

Injuries which can't be healed in time with herbs. My psychic gift however is therapeutic touch. Thanks to that I was able to save her life, too bad she would die sometime after that. Three years after that to be exact."

I had a feeling I knew exactly who this wolf was, "Her name was Ticura wasn't it?"

"Yes it was. She was an Alpha Female."

"I knew that, I'm a member of her pack."

"Oh, well then I'm so sorry for your loss." Athena said sadly.

I was already lost in thought; I wanted to tell her that Ticura's death meant nothing to me since I would not have existed had it not happened, my thoughts kept me silent however. I then realized that I would never be as good as Athena when it came to healing, and neither would the triplets.

TUESDAY APRIL 14, 2020

TODAY THE BOMBERS, archers, and gunners had to fight on the battlefield due to the lack of animals with swords, Tasers, and knives. During this battle we only lost Crispin and Nestor; making Eudorus our only Old One left.

At dinner, my brother Luka finally made the announcement that I was the wolf army's new leader, "Today in my army, I saw a wolf who fought not to maim her enemies but to kill her enemies. Her war tactics were flawless and her fighting skills were dominate to even that of my father Achilles. She may have been an archer but she's proved to be just as fierce as a wolverine. It is for this reason and with the approval of our Old One, that I appoint Mysty as my army's new leader."

I stood up to accept everyone's approving howls, chirps, squeaks, yowls, hisses, and croaks. As I stood I glanced at Flippy who was also howling his approval and I saw a spark of pride in his eyes. It made me beam with such over whelming joy that I'm pretty sure I was glowing. Afterwards, I once again left the city to meet with Athena and tell her the good news. She proudly congratulated me before moving on to more healing tips and herbs.

"Athena, have you ever lost a patient?" I questioned to once again interrupt her ranting.

"Oh. Yes, just once it's still a shameful memory for me, but I'll tell you. I might as well, the triplets know about it as well. It's a very depressing story which will haunt me for the rest of my life, it's the reason I left England. To this day I can never treat another patient without thinking of him."

"Who was he?"

"A wolf pup, he was just a month old. He was so little and cute, but it had been a remarkably harsh winter. In all of my fifteen years I had never seen a winter as harsh as that one before. The wolf pup in fact had been my first patient. His mother had fought her way through a blizzard to find me. She had been to all the other more experienced healers but they rejected her."

"Why would they do that?"

"They didn't want to waste all their herbs on a wolf pup who might not survive." Athena revealed.

"How cruel!"

"Yes it was. She came to me and I instantly accepted them. Her son had a sever pneumonia. I used up nearly all of my stored herbs in the hopes that they would work and he would survive."

"Why didn't you use therapeutic touch?"

"It doesn't work for illnesses only injuries." Athena explained.

"He didn't respond to the herbs?"

"No. If the other healers had taken him in, he would have had a fighting chance since they were closer to his den than I was. The pup died the next night like I knew he would. His mother never blamed me for her pup's death though I think she should have. But she was grateful to me because I tried when no one else would. I had devoted my time, energy, and most of my herbs to her son, and even though he died she thanked me for never giving up on her son."

"Can you treat a sever pneumonia now?"

"That's my dark secret Mysty. As excellent a healer you believe me to be, to this day, I have no idea how to heal a sever pneumonia. And because I don't the triplets don't either."

I hoped no one came down with a case of sever pneumonia during this war.

THURSDAY APRIL 16, 2020

ONLY THE ARCHERS and bombers had to fight on the battlefield today. The gunners were forced to stay inside the city walls because Flippy had to start a fight with Luka. If there's one thing Luka couldn't stand, it was insubordination in any form. A fact that Flippy had not realized until today.

Last night when Luka told us that he wanted me stationed at the front of our army with all of the other army leaders, Flippy had a problem with that. He however waited until the three of us were alone before he started protesting. Since I was an archer and all of the other archers and the gunners were stationed towards the back of the army, Flippy felt I should be back there with them or he should be up there with me since we were partners.

Luka refused to tolerate Flippy's "insubordination" and punished him by stationing the gunners inside the city's walls. Flippy vowed he would always hate Luka after that. Unfortunately today Ajax died. It was hard to lose yet another brother, especially when he was the youngest. Ajax had always been a puppy at heart since he was only two years old, and maybe that's what led to his downfall.

The triplets had their paws full with injured wolves today, and for the first time I was one of them. I had sustained some minor arrow wounds when I let my guard down to try and help Ajax, but he was already dead by the time I reached him. When Flippy noticed my wounds, his hatred towards Luka increased and he lashed out at Luka, blaming him for my injuries.

Luka finally snapped back and snarled, "I don't care about what happens to her, I care about what happens to my pack!"

If Flippy had known my brother as I did, he would have known that Luka didn't actually mean that he didn't care for me, he meant to say that the pack was more important than me. Flippy however was not as fluent in Luka's language as I was.

WEDNESDAY APRIL 22, 2020

THE BATTLE WAS on the seventeenth, but I had been too injured to write. It all started because of the last battle. The gunners were still being forced to stay inside the city which did not help me as I tried to tell Flippy what Luka really meant and that he was a good leader. Flippy however refused to listen to me.

Brutus had fallen for his partner Heather and had become very protective over her, this time it cost him his life. He didn't die on the battlefield like Ajax, but rather from his injuries like Odysseus. Heather soon followed him to Heaven after being shot down by unsympathetic humans. After that Luka decided to station the healers outside the city's walls as well. I would have objected, but even though I was secretly the Alpha Female, Luka was still older than me and therefore more dominant.

Later in the night, Luka called a secret family meeting and I brought Flippy with me since we were very close. Luka ignored the fact that I brought Flippy and began to instantly lash out at us due to the deaths of his youngest brothers, "I can't believe you three! Was losing one younger brother not enough? Was it necessary to lose all three of our younger brothers? The day after we lost our youngest brother, we had to lose our last youngest brother? I can understand why Tiberius and Spartacus did nothing. They were practically born incompetent! As for you Mysty, I expected more!"

I was struck with shock as Luka suddenly began blaming me for Brutus's death. Before I could defend myself, Luka's tongue lashing continued, "You were the one our father expected to follow in his paw steps; you were supposed to be the greatest warrior in the forest!"

"I'm sorry Luka." I mumbled as I looked down at my paws, but Luka was not willing to accept my apology.

"Sorry doesn't bring our brothers back from the grave! If anyone should be sorry, it should be me for choosing you to be the army's leader, I clearly made a mistake. A mistake which cost me the lives of three brothers I had helped to raise since they were puppies. You are just a half-sister who I have only recently had the misfortune of meeting!"

My heart had snapped in two and I left the city immediately to find my mentor hoping that I could confide in her. I could hear Flippy following me the entire time, but I was too fast for him. I then located the road which separated the forest from the battlefield and I picked up my pace but just as I had reached the road, I heard Flippy yell, "Mysty, look out!"

The warning had come too late unfortunately, as I turned my head and saw a pair of bright lights followed by something hitting me, knocking the wind out of me, and causing me to skid across the road. The car continued on its merry way while I was lying in pain and having difficulties breathing. I soon passed out from the pain.

When I had woken up earlier this morning, I was in Athena's tree, the fur on my left side was gone and I had a long gash on my left side with stiches visible along it. Athena greeted me and told me Flippy was waiting for me below to escort me home. Apparently the car hadn't been going very fast and only caused minimal damage, but gave me a deep, nasty gash that had to be stitched.

Luka had not been informed of where Flippy and I were, but he greeted me back warmly which surprised me, but I guess disappearing for five days does that to an animal. Luka allowed me to return to my bedroom so I could rest for the remainder of the day.

SATURDAY APRIL 25, 2020

BEFORE TODAY'S BATTLE, Luka asked if I had felt up to fighting today. I assured him I was, and he responded by assigning Flippy to be my personal body guard for today's battle. I fired back at Luka by pointing out that I was not a helpless pup, until he found it necessary to remind me that I was a pup since I was only seven months old.

I was feeling sore about Luka's decision until I realized that I could in fact fight back, since as the army's leader, I could do a last minute station change. I stationed the archers and gunners in the back once more, including Flippy.

Once the battle started, I noticed that the humans kept on trying to reopen my gash by cutting my stitches. Titan was also fighting with stitches from an injury he had sustained in the last battle, but the humans had managed to cut open his. Luckily the triplets had gotten to him in time to re-stitch him. No human managed to get that close to me without being killed.

At the end of the battle, for the first time since this war started, there were no casualties for the wolf army! Luka commended me and Flippy praised me, but I felt that Athena would like to hear the good news as well, so I once again went to visit her. I cautiously crossed the road, but when I got to the other side, I was shocked to discover that there was no forest; the humans had burned it all to the ground!

I called for Athena, but she never heeded my calls. I ran through the forest, kicking up the ashes that littered the floor as I ran. If they hadn't been grey, I would have sworn that they were snowflakes.

Once I came across the remains of the tree that Athena had called home, I started to see a trail of bloody gold and white feathers. I followed the trail until I came across Athena. My mentor's lifeless body was sprawled amongst the ashes which had turned her once beautiful gold and white feathers to a dark brown color due to her feathers being caked with dried blood and ashes. Her coal black eyes which had at one time sparked with wisdom were now dull and foggy.

I grabbed her body and started to dig a grave for her as I thought about how different she looked. She looked nothing like my mentor due to the state her body was in. Just before I buried her, I noticed the bullet wounds covering her body and realized she must have been shot down as she tried to escape the fire.

I was wrong; my army did lose a valuable member today. I wanted to tell the triplets, but as far as they knew, I had never stepped outside of the city and I wanted to keep my healing lessons from Athena a secret. I couldn't even tell my other friend Slash. The only one I told was Flippy.

TUESDAY APRIL 28, 2020

TONIGHT DURING DINNER I was having my usual conversation with Flippy and Slash when Luka suddenly stood, which ended any and all conversation in the room. As we all stood, I had a feeling I knew exactly what the meeting was going to be about after Luka had told me about what the birds had reported. Luka wasted no time in getting right to the point, "I have a mission for my pack army's leader and her partner."

Flippy and I stepped forward at once and waited to hear what our mission was, "We are running out of warriors and Sandsone, the leader of the bird army, has informed me that in the human's camp they have captured wild wolves. Your mission is to find them and bring them back here where they can help us fight."

"Will they want to?" I felt the need to ask.

"After what the humans have done to them, they'd be fools not to fight." Luka pointed out, "You two will leave immediately tonight."

"Just the two of us?" Flippy questioned.

Luka glared at him and growled, but kept calm as he explained, "Two are less noticeable than five. I think two will be enough, especially when you have the brave and fierce Mysty with you."

Flippy and I exchanged a glance before we said goodbye to Slash and left the city.

The human's camp was very close to the city. While the forest was just north of the city, the human's camp was east of the city across the large gorge which separated the human's camp from the city's battlefield. It was surrounded by a chain link fence that stretched all the way around their territory, razor wire was wrapped around the top of the fence, there were four humans with rifles stationed in each corner of the fence, and there was a humming sound coming from the fence that warned me the fence was electric as well.

"How will we get in?" Flippy whispered.

"I'll dig a hole in the north side, it has a blind spot. The humans will never see it coming."

"Do you see the captured wolves?" Flippy asked.

"No, but I think I can hear them over towards the east side." I said quietly as I began to dig at the bottom of the fence, taking care not to touch the electrocuted metal.

When I had finally made a hole large enough I squeezed in first while Flippy followed. I decided that once we found and released the wolves, Flippy would lead them to the exit while I held the humans back, and once Flippy gave me the signal I would retreat with them. Tonight the humans proved to not only be incredibly gullible but also ridiculously stupid. They as I said, "Never saw it coming". Flippy and I returned to the city in almost no time.

Upon re-entering the city, we handed over the escaped wolves to Luka before we retired to our own rooms for the night. God knows how much I needed to sleep.

WEDNESDAY APRIL 29, 2020

I HAVE NOW become the older sister of a coyote pup. I'll start from the beginning and work my way up to the unfortunate part.

Luka had just introduced the freed captives to the rest of the pack. Only two were dogs and one of course was a coyote pup, but the rest were all wolves.

Duchess was the coyote pup. I could tell from the moment she looked at me with those huge blue eyes that she was going to cause me nothing but trouble. She was only a month old, but I had never been fond of pups and today would have been no different if not for a little problem that Luka would later point out to me.

I started pairing up the new comers and assigning weapons which I thought would be simple enough even though I hardly knew any of them. I paired them off based on my gut instinct. Since Duchess was just a pup, I left her out.

After that I felt that my job was done and I had chosen

their weapons and partners fairly well and I was proud of myself. I was just about to leave to let the senior warriors help train the new comers how to use their weapons, when I was stopped by Luka who had with him, Duchess. She was trailing behind him as shy as a salmon around a pack of bears. I still greeted my brother warmly if not a little cautiously, "Hello Luka, what's with the pup? She's too young to train."

"She thinks you're related since you share the same fur color."

"That's ridiculous!" I snorted.

"Let's just humor her for now, she's just a pup, and she's a Lab Pet Survivor."

"A Lab Pet? You want me to put up with a pup who could have unforetold mental and physical health problems?"

"It's just to help her adapt. When she gets comfortable enough the triplets can examine her and see if there's anything wrong with her. She doesn't have to live in your room, just close enough to feel secure."

"Fine, but just until she's comfortable."

Luka grinned at me and pushed the pup over to me. I was not impressed by the scrap of fur that was presented to me, but I figured that if she was fit to fight, I could mentor her. So I humored her false belief and allowed her the room across the hall from mine. I spent the day showing Duchess around and despite my skepticism today I think she could make a fine apprentice.

SUNDAY MAY 3, 2020

I HAVE JUST become Luka's last sibling. We fought again today and lost Tiberius and Spartacus.

I didn't know how Luka would respond to their deaths, so I tried to avoid him for the rest of the day, which was easy enough. I just spent the day with the newer members of the army and of course with Duchess right behind me the entire time.

I just watched them practice with their weapons and instructed Duchess to do so as well just so she could study the training I would soon put her through. As I watched them, I noticed Rambo trotting up to me, "When will you announce the new partners?" Rambo asked.

"During dinner." I decided.

"I know you already know my name, but we haven't been properly introduced, I'm Rambo."

"You may already know my name as well, I'm Mysty and this skinny little scrap of fur is Duchess, my soon to be apprentice."

Just then, the she-wolf Auburn came up to me as well, "Oh and this is my lovely mate Auburn." Rambo introduced her as well.

"Mate huh? A little young for mates don't you think?" I grinned.

"That coming from the wolf fawning over that dog, what was his name again? It was um... Flippy! That's right!" Auburn dawned on it.

"Well I guess when the right one comes along." I shrugged, "How did you two meet?"

"We were stealing our food from the same deli. There I was ripping carcasses off the meat hooks when suddenly I look over, and there's the most beautiful wolf I ever seen attacking the deli human. I had never seen a wolf who could match my viciousness and stealth when it came to attacking a human."

"We didn't hit it off well at first. He asked me out, I told him to drop dead and stop stealing my meat, but when the security humans came we ended up fighting back to back. At first I wasn't pleased, but when our pelts touched we felt a spark between us and well you know how that is." Auburn finished.

I thought it was an interesting story and just like that, we hit it off. I now have two new friends, well two if you don't count Duchess.

MONDAY MAY 4, 2020

LAST NIGHT I had reassigned partners for those who had lost theirs. Today however was another battle.

As I was leaving the city with the army, I couldn't help but notice Luka staring at me as if he wanted to stop me from going out there but knew he couldn't. I realized that it must be him reacting to the deaths of all of his brothers, but I would not allow myself to be distracted by him, I had to do my duty to my pack.

Now that the battle is over, I wish that he had. We had to end in a retreat and I was shot twice, they were only grazes but they were still very sore and painful. I was shot in my left hip and shoulder before we retreated. I felt stupid for having called for the retreat, but when I saw more humans coming in from the horizon; I thought retreating was our best bet.

I waited patiently as Sherry patched me up. Luka was curious about my condition, but Sherry assured him that I was fine. While I checked among my ranks for any casualties, I was both pleased and surprised to find none, but many of my warriors were gravely injured. Maybe it had been a good thing for me to call for that retreat after all.

I still wasn't sure so I wanted to ask Luka, but I had always found Luka unapproachable. I thought about asking Flippy, but it seemed like a ridiculous question to be asking him since he had about as much battle experience as I did, that was true for Slash as well. I figured maybe Sherry would be able to tell me until I recalled that she was a healer and not a fighter, she probably wouldn't have known. I did think about asking Duchess, but that would have been even more ridiculous than asking Sherry, Slash, Flippy, or Luka.

Luckily for me, my eyes caught Rambo, if anyone had any battle training it would be Rambo, I could tell by the way he trained and fought that he had more training than he let on to. I decided he would be the best one to ask, so I did. I walked right up to him and asked, "Was that a good idea? Calling for a retreat I mean."

Rambo looked at me funny and simply questioned my doubt.

I explained to him that while there were no fatalities today, I was worried that my other warriors would not have agreed with the retreat and may even hate me for it.

"Well they can't always like you." Rambo pointed out, "And as for the retreat, you did what you thought was the right thing to do. If you keep on questioning yourself your warriors will start to do the same."

I took comfort in his words of wisdom, at the same time that question still rang in my ears. Maybe I was meant to be a healer after all. I wished Athena was still alive, I could have asked her.

SATURDAY MAY 9, 2020

TODAY WAS THE worst battle I have ever fought! We once again had to end in a retreat, but this time it was because of my love for Flippy.

In the heat of the battle with all the humans, I noticed I couldn't see Flippy or any of my other fighters for that matter. I searched endlessly for Flippy until I finally found him lying on the battle field covered in patches of blood. The triplets were on the other side of the battlefield, but thankfully Slash was nearby, "Go get Sherry, Flippy's hurt."

"Where are they? I can't see anything but humans!" Slash howled.

"I think I'm going to have to call another retreat, the battlefield is too crowded."

"Again?" Slash whined.

"Now Slash! Flippy's dying!" I snapped.

Slash took her cue and swiftly vanished into the swarm of fighting humans to find Sherry. I protected Flippy as

I waited anxiously for Sherry. Sherry arrived about five minutes later but Slash was nowhere to be seen. I wasted no time in calling a retreat and I followed close behind Sherry as she retreated with Flippy in tow. I even caught Carry running while dragging Slash with her which did explain why she had not returned with Sherry

I too had sustained some minor wounds of my own which Cherry had patched up for me, but I was bitterly angry that I had let my love blind me to winning the battle. However since there were so many humans and so few warriors on the battlefield today due to yesterday's battle maybe once again, the retreat was not a terrible idea. We had already lost several warriors anyway. Who knows how many more we would have lost?

SUNDAY MAY 10, 2020

LAST NIGHT THE clinic burned down and it took Slash with it.

I had assigned Tyler the duty of night sentry, but with Flippy and Slash in the clinic, I didn't feel tired enough to sleep so I decided to sit out on my balcony. As I was staring up at the sky, I saw a large ball of fire fly over the walls of the city. I ran outside and followed the smell of smoke to the clinic which had been hit by the fire ball. I took action immediately, "Tyler what caused this?"

"A catapult." he reported.

"Rambo! Auburn! Go disable the catapult before they take another shot at us. Sicily and Nica be ready to close the roof hatch if you see them about to load another fire ball. Sherry, did everyone get out of the clinic?"

"No, Cherry's still in there with Slash and Flippy."

As soon as I heard that, I forgot about everything else around me and I dashed in there to find Flippy. I found him in the hall just opposite of where Cherry and Slash were trapped. I wanted to save my friend, but I needed Flippy more. I chose to save Flippy instead of Slash and Cherry. Once I started dragging Flippy away from the fire, I saw a loose beam collapse and encase Cherry and Slash in the hall. I wasted no time in pulling Flippy out of the building. When I turned and looked behind me, I saw Cherry leap out the burning doors of the clinic before the entire building collapsed.

I sat beside Flippy and watched as the building burned hoping Slash would somehow miraculously come running out of the building as well, but she never did. I called Cherry to me to explain what happened to Slash. Cherry told me that when the beam collapsed, Slash pushed Cherry out through a small opening at the bottom and when Cherry tried to pull Slash out from under the beam, the rest of the ceiling in the hall collapsed and buried Slash. I howled tragically at the death of my best friend. Slash was only eight months old.

Rambo and Auburn reported their success at burning down the human's catapult, but I was in no mood for celebrating. My best friend had just tragically died because of me and I just wanted to go back to my room and forget that the last thing I ever did to Slash was snap at her. I missed her already.

THURSDAY MAY 14, 2020

I FOUND MYSELF stuck in my room all day and night as I tried to forget about Slash's horrible death, but the images of the last moment I saw her wouldn't leave my mind. Flippy came to me today and suggested I start training Duchess to take my mind off of it. I decided to take his advice since Duchess was old enough to begin training and because misery loves company.

I took Duchess out to the battlefield and started off with the simpler attack and defensive moves. Unfortunately, she conquered none of them. She couldn't even execute the maneuvers properly. Once noon hit, I decided to take a break. The entire time we trained she dodged only one of my halfhearted blows while never landing any herself.

While we took our break, I decided to tell her about psychic abilities since she was too young to have developed hers yet. I told her about my ability of bilocation, my mother's ability to see into the near future, and Flippy's ability to determine the strength of any creature in battle which was why he rarely lost to an opponent.

"What's mine?" Duchess asked.

"I don't know. You're still too young, but you'll figure it out very soon. It'll just hit you."

Duchess was about to ask another question when she spotted something. I turned and came face to face with a silver wolf with green eyes who was about four inches taller than me. I had never seen her before. She had large muscles rippling under her pelt, and her silver fur was bristled with hostility, her green eyes glowing with maliciousness. I knew instantly that she was one of the humans' pets and at the moment her blood hungry eyes were fixated on Duchess.

The wolf was obviously stronger than I was, but Duchess would never stand a chance against the humongous wolf who could swallow her whole. I stepped protectively in front of Duchess and bristled my fur as I began to growl a warning at the wolf. I could sense Duchess right behind me shrinking herself until she practically was invisible.

The wolf seemed pleased with my decision to protect my "little sister" and I knew that it was about to turn into a blood bath and possibly my funeral. I focused on my target; we circled each other a few times, to size up the other before the fight began.

She was strong but I was swift. I jumped on top of her

and bit into her spine; she stood on her hind legs and fell back. Her sudden weight knocked the wind out of me but I forced myself up. She made an advancement towards Duchess but I grabbed a knife from the battlefield and threw it at the she-wolf. It hit her right shoulder blade, but she yanked it out as if it were nothing more than a thorn.

She then wasted no time in leaping at a gun she found behind a boulder and began shooting at me. I dodged the bullets until she ran out and had to drop the gun. I jumped at her but she kicked me in midair, I however managed to regain my balance and executed a backflip instead.

In a fury, she tackled me to the ground and pulled out a knife of her own. I hit her repeatedly in the face and tried to squirm away, but she was still too strong for me. I decided to use my swift reflexes to rip the knife out of her paw and I tried to stab her until she hit me in the face as well. I head butted her in the nose and she reeled off of me, but I dropped the knife.

Instead of trying to retrieve the knife, she hit me so hard I flew back and hit the city's walls. At that time I realized that the silver wolf was a great fighter, but I was better. I used my stored up energy to charge at the she wolf and I head butted her in the chest so hard that I heard many of her ribs snap. I used her sudden pain as a distraction to grab Duchess and run back into the city. The she-wolf did not follow us.

Once inside, I groomed myself while I tried to settle my nerves. I told Duchess not to tell Flippy about my encounter with the silver wolf. While I managed to hide my true feelings from Duchess, I must admit that the whole experience left me very shaken up.

FRIDAY MAY 15, 2020

LUKA DECIDED TO have another battle today even though Sherry tried to advise him against having another battle with no medical supplies. Eudoras however, had other plans and Luka chose his wisdom over Sherry's. I obeyed my brother's orders even though it meant the death of many of our warriors.

After five intense hours, I decided to call for another retreat, much to my warriors' dismay. When I realized we had lost fourteen of our warriors, I knew I did the right thing. I had never before lost so many warriors.

Luka decided to make another announcement that evening in the Meal Hall, "Due to the lack of medical supplies, I am sending a patrol of wolves to secure some from the humans. Mysty, as the army's leader, I expect you to be willing to lead such a patrol."

I stepped forward to accept my new mission before Luka continued, "And to show the humans that revenge is a dish best served with a cold heart, I want you and your patrol to send a message to the humans, 'you burn our clinic, we burn yours', and I want you to burn their clinic to the ground! After gathering the medical supplies of course."

"Luka, with all due respect, doing that would violate our morals. Killing on the battlefield is one thing, but burning down their clinic would mean the death of many defenseless humans." I tried to sway him away from the revengeful plot.

The room then erupted with both voices who agreed and disagreed with me but the other armies stayed out of it. They knew it was our debate not theirs.

"Good! Then this war will end sooner!" I heard Sicily snarl.

"No Mysty's right! We are better than this!" Emily yipped.

"It's not like we're burning down a nursery!" Thistle growled.

"How long until it comes to that?!" Sherry demanded.

"This is only a retaliation; we have the right to defend ourselves!" Rose tried to convince them.

"Their clinic could be full of defenseless humans!" Shakespeare reminded us.

"So was our clinic! And they burned it down in cold blood! Eudorus said swiftly.

"It would just show the humans that we are no better than they are!" Margalow pointed out.

"We are much greater than they are! And we shall prove it by showing them that animals are a force to be reckoned with!" Carry announced.

"It's not like they were purposefully aiming for the clinic! Two wrongs don't make a right!" Nica fought.

"I believe you're all aware of my position." Rambo said darkly and I knew he wasn't talking in favor of the humans.

"Silence!" Luka demanded. The room was instantly quieted, "This is not a debate, and I have made my decision. Mysty will take Keekers, Char, and Coraltin to the humans' clinic and they shall do their duty to their pack."

"Luka, please don't make me do this." I whispered to him.

"This is not a debate." Luka reminded me.

I tried to persuade him that God would not be pleased, but he dismissed me just like he did to Sherry.

I met up with my group members and watched as Flippy dashed after Luka to clash heads with him once more. I tried on my saddlebag just like the others and then got a list of medical supplies from the triplets. Before we left I handed Duchess over to a flustered and volatile Flippy so he could watch after her while I was gone. He happily agreed to, but I could tell he was still sore at Luka.

I retrieved my bow and arrows while Char grabbed the gasoline and lighter needed to set the clinic on fire.

SATURDAY MAY 16, 2020

THE MISSION STARTED out well. We struck the humans' camp just before dawn when they would least expect it. The hole I had dug the last time I was there with Flippy was still untouched as if the humans had never even noticed it. I actually started to feel sorry for the poor brainless creatures.

Once we were all on the other side of the fence I started to give them instructions, "Coraltin has the list, so I want you three to sneak in undetected and nab all the medical supplies we need, but don't let your saddlebags weigh you down, we'll have to jump over that gorge again and while the river may still be frozen, I'm pretty sure that's very thin ice on the surface."

I lead my group towards the clinic while still keeping the hole under the fence in sight. I sniffed out the clinic and alerted all of my senses for any sign of humans, but it was all clear. I swung my tail to the left side as the signal for them to move in while I stood watch. When they came out of the clinic I told them to start making their way back while I did the dirty deed. Char had already poured the gasoline all over the clinic and eagerly handed me the lighter.

I pulled out one of my arrows and lit it with the lighter before I shot it at the clinic. I repeated this action seven more times until their clinic was completely engulfed in flames just like ours was.

I started to walk back to the hole, when I heard someone coming around the corner, and discovered to my horror that it was the silver wolf. I couldn't believe my eyes, I must have broken about four or five of her ribs and yet there she was! After two days she seemed to be perfectly fine and healed. When I saw her eyes light up with the urge to kill, I began a mad gallop to the hole under the fence while the silver wolf remained hot on my heels.

I knew that the hole was slightly too small for her to fit through, but even that only gave me a five second head start as I dashed through the hole and ran to the gorge. I noticed that my group was already waiting for me on the other side which made me pick up my pace as the gorge came closer into view. It was a five yard jump so I knew I had to use up the last of my adrenaline to make it across.

I leapt into the air and was about half way across when the sliver wolf shot me with an arrow in my right shoulder. It knocked me off balance and I lost my concentration. Before I realized it, I was missing the other side of the gorge and falling, just barely missing the edge. I suddenly stopped falling because something had grabbed my scruff. I looked up and was surprised to see Flippy holding on to my scruff, I also noticed that half of him was hanging over the side as well and he was slipping due to the mud on the ground.

I knew what I had to do, "Flippy, you have to let me go!"

"No, the ice will crack and you'll drown if you don't go down the falls first!" he said in a muffled voice.

"One life lost isn't as bad as two lives lost just drop me!" I begged recalling how I had made the same choice not too long ago.

"No, I'm not going to let you go!"

"Why?" I demanded.

"I... I just can't do it!" Flippy said in a very frustrated voice.

I had found a way to end the dilemma by biting him sharply on the nose. He instinctively released me before realizing he had done so. He howled as I fell and hit the ice. I landed in my left side to prevent the arrow from going in any further.

My left side was jarred, but I didn't suffer from any broken bones and to my amazement, the ice didn't crack. I slowly stood up but upon doing so I noticed that the ice had cracked from my impact after all and the sudden shift in weight was enough to get the rest of the ice to shatter.

The river became alive and angry; a wild wave came up from behind me and knocked me under the water. I fought against the rapids to try and resurface, but I had never been a strong swimmer and the frigid temperature of the water wasn't helping. I heard something coming closer to me and saw that Flippy was once again trying to save me. Flippy grabbed me by the scruff again and fought against the currant. We somehow managed to make it to the other side of the river bank.

I laid there for a while shivering as I spit and coughed out a few mouthfuls of water. Flippy continued to nudge me along back to the city. As it turns out Luka had sent him, Rambo, and Emily to see if there were any other animals being held captive. They never found any that night.

SUNDAY MAY 17, 2020

TODAY WAS THE first battle that I had missed out on due to the arrow wound I had received from the silver wolf. Luka decided to appoint Flippy as the temporary leader of the army. I didn't want to miss out on the fight, but I knew I'd be no use on the battlefield if I was too hurt to focus, so against my resilient will, I stayed in my room.

Hours after the battle had gone by and I could hear Duchess outside my door, but Rambo kept on shooing her away with offers of training her battle tactics, but sometimes he had to resort to the promise of a treat. As much as I loved Duchess, she was still in the annoying stage of her life, and while I was hurt, that was the last thing I needed.

Flippy finally came into my room after dinner to report how that fight went. We were victorious today, but we lost Cherry.

When I asked how Cherry died, Flippy told me it was due to a bomb one of the humans had set near where

Linger was injured and Cherry was trying to tend to him. I felt terrible about poor Cherry's death, but I know that none of the fatalities were my fault; it was just their time to die.

Despite my realization I did feel that Slash died for nothing.

WEDNESDAY MAY 20, 2020

I HAD ALMOST completely healed, but Luka decided it would be best if I missed one more battle just to be sure. I was reluctant to agree but I had recently developed a nasty headache which refused to leave me alone. I knew Luka was probably right and I decided to trust Flippy again with the army.

As I was lying there alone, I realized that a combination of my disturbing encounters with the silver wolf, along with my injury, and my depression from Slash's death had caused me to forget to reassign partners to those who had lost theirs, and I was pretty sure neither Luka nor Flippy had reassigned them. Unfortunately there was nothing I could do about it now.

When Flippy came to see me, he reported that several others had died. I was very disappointed in myself for being so absent minded. I worry that I may have been responsible in at least some slight involvement with their deaths. Flippy pointed out that lately the battlefield has become too polluted with humans for partners to matter much, but still I should have known better. Or maybe I should have seen it coming, after all last time Rambo had to remind me.

My headache had caused me to make another diary entry brief once more! It was feeling a little better though.

FRIDAY MAY 22, 2020

MY SHOULDER HAD thankfully healed by the time some new recruits had surprised us. Apparently they lived south of us in a small forest of their own until the humans decided to clear cut it. They were of course welcomed additions to the army.

Luka spent some time with them before he turned them over to me so I could pair them up and assign them weapons. I once again relied on my gut instinct since I didn't know if I would have enough time to get to know them before the next battle.

There were only two left, a pup about Duchess' age and a large tawny wolf with violet red eyes. I instantly recognized her from Luka's descriptions; there was no doubt in my mind that it was my twin sister, "Missi!" I gawked at her mysterious return.

Missi greeted me warmly but before I could get another word in, Luka pushed me aside to welcome his favorite sister back. As they chatted Flippy stood beside me while glaring at Luka. I felt left out as usual, but I knew that Luka had the right to be happy that his sister returned after all these months.

"Duchess told me about the silver wolf."

"I told her not to." I growled bitterly.

"I think Missi is the silver wolf." Flippy cautioned.

"Impossible. The wolf was silver with green eyes, Missi is tawny with violet red eyes, and the silver wolf was taller."

Flippy was not convinced but Auburn and Rambo interrupted any further conversation between us. I then noticed that Auburn looked pregnant. I instantly commented on this and they happily confirmed it. I reminded them that it meant I would have to pull Auburn out of the battle until her pups were born and weaned, but she assured me that she could still fight since they weren't due for a while.

I wasn't sure I agreed with this, but Luka stopped me from debating the matter by reminding me that I still hadn't assigned weapons. My mind was whirling with all of these events but I remained calm on the outside as I assigned the new group their weapons.

I got right to it and assigned weapons to the new warriors and made sure to give Missi the bow and arrows as a weapon hoping that it would be a way for us to reconnect. But I paired her with Dapple since Lola died.

SATURDAY MAY 23, 2020

TODAY WE LOST six warriors. The cowardly human army decided to wait until night to strike. I think it was pay back for the two times I broke into their camp at night to raid it.

It happened at about almost two in the morning. I woke up to the sound of the warning bell going off and sure enough, there was the army. We fought until the humans retreated which happened sometime after six in the morning.

As tired as I was Missi kept me up by telling me about the story of how she had escaped. She had apparently been trying to escape for months, which she had managed to do some time before Flippy and I freed the other captives. She tried to remember where the pack lived but everything looked so different so she just went with her instincts and headed south. She didn't find our pack, but she found another pack and had lived with them for a while until the pack moved into the city.

I felt that her story confirmed that she couldn't have been the silver wolf; she had been living down south the entire time.

Since tomorrow would mark our eight month birthday, I decided spending the rest of the morning finishing my hours of sleep would be the best way to get to my birthday sooner.

SUNDAY MAY 31, 2020

I HAD BEEN dog-napped last night. The silver wolf had somehow managed to get into my room and she tied me up while I was sleeping and dragged me out of the city and away from the battle field. She continued to drag me until we came to an oak tree. She then started to raise me from the ground until I was hanging from the tree like a piñata.

I struggled against my bonds, I knew that I could escape if I could get my paws untangled enough to slip out of the knots. The silver wolf however had returned with a knife and sliced a long my flank where the scar from my stiches still remained. She seemed to get some kind of sick pleasure out of cutting me and did it again by slicing across my left shoulder blade, "I've been waiting for this since the day I met you." she said just before she held the knife up to land a killing stab.

Just before she came down on my flank with the knife, a gun shot went off and hit her paw. She howled in pain and dropped the knife before turning to see Flippy. Once she saw him, the silver wolf ran ten meters away before she froze suddenly and turned in our direction. We were waiting for her next move, but she stayed still.

I took the moment to slither out of the ropes and fell out of the tree. Flippy came up to me to check and see if I was alright. When I assured him I was we began slowly advancing on the silver wolf. I was expecting her to move any second, but she was still as a stature the entire time we were crawling up to her.

When we were about five meters away from her, she suddenly became alive again and was standing on her hind legs with a large white orb in her paws. Before either of us could act, the orb flew right out of her paws and hit me. It sank into my body and I howled in sudden pain as I realized it was draining my energy. It was an energy orb, that was her psychic ability which was why she had healed so fast. She was stealing energy from me to heal her paw.

The orb quickly soared out of me and the silver wolf absorbed the orb and Flippy and I watched as her paw healed before our eyes. Once her paw had healed the silver wolf dashed away before Flippy could even try to advance on her again.

Flippy helped me up and I leaned against him for support as we made our way back to the city. Flippy got Sherry to stitch up my new knife wounds before I returned to my room except that time I locked the door behind me. As I would be doing from then on.

THURSDAY JUNE 4, 2020

WE HAD ANOTHER battle today, but just before the battle, Missi came up to me and asked me for another combat knife, I asked her what happened to the one she had picked up from the battle field and she told me that it was stolen the last time we fought the humans. I found her another knife, but reminded her that her main weapon still had to be the bow and arrows since it was the weapon I had assigned her.

After the battle, I was walking through the city in the dead of night and almost bumped into Eudorus. "Oh, Eudorus I'm sorry I almost bumped into you."

"As well as you should be, but you are just the mutt I've been looking for."

"Why?" I asked, not sure what he wanted.

"Don't you think it's odd that Luka's half-sister looks a lot like you?"

"Does she? I hadn't noticed, but I'm sure it's just a lovely coincidence."

"Perhaps." Eudorus was clearly not convinced, he was an old wolf, but he wasn't stupid.

Eudorus stared at me for a long time before he retreated back into the shadows. I suppressed a shiver and decided to return to my room. I sat on my balcony and watched the moon. I wasn't there long before I felt that I was not alone. I turned and saw Flippy beside me. I said the first thing that came to my mind, "Eudorus is on to me."

"Don't let him intimidate you. He may have his suspicions, but that's all he has. Flippy reminded me. I took comfort in Flippy's statement, but my worries would not simply die. I needed more than that.

MONDAY JUNE 13, 2020

TRAGEDY HAS STRUCK today. It all started in the middle of battle, as I was fighting, I saw Rambo and Auburn being chased into the western woods by a small group of soldiers. Realizing that they would need my help I followed them.

I tracked down the humans, Rambo, and Auburn, but Rambo had killed all the human soldiers. I was about to congratulate him, when I noticed something was wrong with Auburn. Thanks to Athena's training I soon dawned on the fact that Auburn was going into premature labor. I knew that there was no time to go back for Sherry, and Rambo would never leave Auburn, so I revealed my secret training to Rambo as I moved to deliver Auburn's pups.

By the time I had helped Auburn deliver her first pup, a black furred male, Flippy had found us. I handed the pup to Rambo to lick clean while I tried to order Flippy to get Sherry, but Auburn started giving birth to her next pup and I knew that there would be no time for Flippy to get Sherry. I gave the next pup, an auburn female, to Flippy to lick clean and tried to save Auburn, but the premature birth had caused her to hemorrhage and with the wounds she had already sustained from battle, she didn't stand a chance. There was blood everywhere, I tried so hard to stop her from bleeding her life out, but I failed.

Upon realizing that I had lost the fight for Auburn's life, I stopped suddenly and turned slowly in Rambo's direction. He looked at me almost pleadingly; I look a deep breath before I sadly announced Auburn's death. Rambo looked in horrid disbelief before howling in such pain and agony that I'm sure even the trees felt it.

Rambo then dashed away with tears in his eyes, I knew that he shouldn't be left alone so I followed after him. I left the pups with Flippy and tore after Rambo. I followed his scent to the creek where I finally found him staring at the water. He knew I was there and said, "After that raid on the deli, she took me back here. I didn't know why until I saw her jump into the water, I thought she fell. There was a waterfall up ahead so I jumped in to save her. As it turns out, the water fall was two feet tall and she was trying to catch a trout. We shared a good laugh about that before I caught an even larger trout. We shared it that night and we lived by the creek ever since then. When we were captured, she was so worried she would never see the creek again. Thanks for giving us our freedom, no matter how brief it was. You should have seen the way she lit up when she saw the creek again."

Before I could even tell him how much his pups needed him, he rose and ran back to where we had left Flippy and the pups. Rambo made it there before I did, but when I turned around the tree I saw Rambo looking at his sleeping pups. Flippy offered to carry Auburn's body back to the city, but Rambo refused his offer and grabbed her himself. Flippy grabbed the black pup and I took the auburn pup. The only wolf we lost that day was Auburn; our battle had been a victory.

Sherry checked out the premature pups, they were so small; they were only as big as my paw. Sherry took the pups away to the new clinic but said that they should be fine.

Auburn's mourning would be held tomorrow, but I just wanted to go back to my room and forget the nightmare of a day I had. Rambo however stopped me, "Mysty, my pups need a mother figure, and since you delivered them, I was hoping you would be their mother figure. I'm not asking you to be my mate, no one will ever be able to replace Auburn, but I want you to be there for them in a way that only a mother can be."

"I'd be honored to be their mother figure. Have you named them?"

"Auburn wanted to name them, so I chose the names she had picked out. The male is Artticus and the female is Athicus."

I nodded at Rambo before I entered my room.

SUNDAY JUNE 14, 2020

WE HELD AUBURN'S mourning today. It was a sad and somber event given Auburn's tragically short life. Rambo decided to have her buried by their creek.

I kept an eye on the pups while Rambo left to bury his mate alone. The pups were adorable and were getting stronger every hour.

When Rambo returned I handed over the pups to him. Rambo clinged to his pups and I understood why, they were all he had. I knew what that was like. The only family I had left were my brother and sister, but I always looked at Rambo as the brother I never had but wished I did.

THURSDAY JULY 2, 2020

FLIPPY HAD BEEN right all along. If I had listened to him in the first place, all of what happened could have been avoided, but my love for my sister had prevented me from seeing her for who she really was, and it nearly cost me my life.

On the 17th of June, we had another battle. The battle was quickly halted however when Missi out of nowhere, joined the human's side and to prove her loyalty, she grabbed her war partner, Dapple, and murdered her. She then revealed herself to be a spy for the humans as well as admitting that she was indeed the silver wolf. She had just painted her fur and placed green contacts in her eyes, and she only looked shorter than the silver wolf because the silver wolf's fur was spiked due to the paint.

After this shock, the humans were easily able to over-power our army and Missi caught me with a barbed wire trap she set up. The humans took over for Missi and began taking me away. I tried to fight them off, but they had me. Flippy tried to free me, but Missi Tazered him and didn't stop until he had passed out. The humans dragged me away while my pack was forced to watch, including Luka and Rambo.

I couldn't understand how something so horrible could have happened; she was my sister, my blood, my twin! How could she have betrayed me? I was scared, I didn't know the sick evil that lurked in my sister's dark and twisted mind, but if she could kill her own war partner without remorse, what chance did I stand? Knowing Luka, he would not fight for my freedom, but I knew that Rambo and Flippy would.

The humans took me to their base and didn't even wait to try to turn me into one of their pet slaves. They apparently used torture to turn animals into slaves, and Missi was all too happy to torture me herself. She showed no mercy for her twin sister. She beat me, drowned me, strangled me, and even resorted to electrocution. She referred to it as "electro shock therapy" since "all disobedient pets had to be shocked back into obedience". Through it all, I would not give in, so she decided to kick it up a notch.

She started using her energy orbs on me. She would take all my energy while leaving me just enough to stay alive. By this time I knew she had no intention of turning me into a pet, she just wanted to torture me to death and I knew she would.

On the 30th of June I was certain that tomorrow's torture would kill me so I hoped that I would die before Missi could kill me. To my surprise, that night I was awoken by a noise. I tried to bilocate, but the torture had weakened me and I could not. My eyes were too tired and refused to open, so I could only hear what was going on. I heard an alarm sound, and my cage door had been opened. I felt something warm touch my left forearm, it reached my left shoulder blade and felt the scar there left behind by Missi from the night she had first captured me. It was clear that whoever it was, they were looking for that scar. I tried to get the scent of the creature, but I could only smell my own blood.

"I found her, she's still alive!" the creature announced. I may have been unable to smell the creature, but I could recognize Flippy's voice instantly.

I heard more paw steps and then Rambo's voice, "We have to get out of here now, they've just released Missi!"

Flippy grabbed me by the scruff and charged away with me while Rambo followed behind.

"Did you find her?" Sherry panted.

"Yes, but they've got Missi coming after us!" Rambo stopped briefly to fill Sherry in.

Sherry lead the way from then on to the fence, Flippy was just behind her while Rambo stayed in the back to cover our escape. I was just happy to be with Flippy again,

I was even more happy when I realized our escape had been a success. Missi couldn't follow us into the city because the tunnel entrance had been switched to a new tunnel.

THURSDAY JULY 9, 2020

I SAVED RAMBO'S life, and last night I watched him leave.

Last night I heard the pups giggling and squeaking so I opened my door and saw Rambo leading his pups away. I followed them out of the city and by the creek. Before Rambo could make his next move I revealed myself.

Rambo's pups took one look at me and squealed, "Mysty! Are you gonna play this game too?"

"What game little ones?" I questioned.

"Daddy told us that we're gonna play 'escape the city' it's really fun!" Artticus yipped.

"Escape the city? Why would you want to do that?"

"Daddy said that there's more to explore than just the city and he's gonna show us." Athicus agreed.

"Really?" I asked rhetorically as I finally looked at Rambo.

Rambo avoided my gaze and said, "Pups, go play in that nearby bush while I talk to Mysty."

The pups obeyed and Rambo walked up to me as I

instantly demanded to know what was going on.

"Mysty, today I was almost stabbed to death. I realized I was all my pups had left. If I died they wouldn't have anyone. I could die before this war ends, even worse, my pups might be old enough to fight if this war continues. I could lose one of my pups or they could lose me. I can't let that happen, so we must leave."

"Where will you go?"

"The coast, it's one of the safest places left."

"But Rambo, you're one of our greatest fighters you can't leave."

"It's for that very reason that I have to leave. I never met your father Achilles, but from what I heard he was the greatest fighter in the forest, and yet he died. So how long till I die or even you?"

"But we need you."

"No, you'll be fine without me." Rambo insisted I knew he wasn't going to change his mind.

Rambo called his pups to him and they were instantly by his side. Rambo lead them across the creek by showing them how to use the stepping stones. Before he could vanish in the bushes on the other side, I called to him in one last desperate plea for him to stay. He just stood there for a few seconds staring at me before he plunged into the undergrowth. I stayed on the other side of the creek for a while, wondering what I should do. There was something about what Rambo said that impacted me, but I couldn't make sense of it.

SATURDAY JULY 11, 2020

THE LEADER OF the bird army, Sandsone, had discovered the location of the general of the human army, but he was stationed on top of the mountains. Luka was not deterred by this; he was determined to end this war as soon as possible.

Luka sent me, Flippy, Eudorus, Flame, Thistle, Thorn, Darkness, and Ghost to the mountains; he figured they were all I would need to take down the human general.

I noticed that Flippy looked ill, but Luka refused to spare him from duty so I was forced to take him along. I also decided to take my diary since I didn't know how long I would be gone.

By sunrise we arrived at the base of the mountains and I had my small group stop for the day, I told them that we would continue on tomorrow but for now we had to prepare ourselves.

I took this opportunity to check on Flippy, he looked even worse, but he still maintained that spark of energy. I knew he loved to fight, but even he had his limits. Would he be even sicker by tomorrow?

SUNDAY JULY 12, 2020

THE INVASION WAS a failure thanks to Eudorus who gave away our position by tripping over a sleeping human.

When the invasion began, we had crept into the tent, but Eurdous tripped over a human and landed on another sleeping human. The humans bolted awake and sounded the alarm.

My pack mates fought the humans, but we were panicked and separated. I quickly decided upon a hasty retreat down the mountain.

One of the humans knew we were retreating and set off a large bomb to purposely cause an avalanche. We could not out run the avalanche and it caught us all in its grasp.

I dug my way out and looked around me. I saw Eudorus, Thorn, and Thistle rise out of the snow, but the rest were missing.

I sniffed out where Flippy had been buried and

dug him out. Thistle and Thorn recovered Ghost and Darkness, but they had been killed in the avalanche, just like Flame had when we later found her body.

We headed back down the mountain, but Flippy hadn't fully recovered and I had to drag him behind me. When Eudorus noticed that Flippy was slowing us down he demanded that I leave him behind. I boldly refused and due to my insubordination to my elder, Eudorus and I fought for domination.

I had to admit, the old wolf still had some impressive fighting moves, but in the end, I had won. That victory did come with a price. When Eudorus had nipped at my throat, he exposed my gem. Every one saw it, including Eudorus who felt the need to give a victory speech, "I knew it! I knew she was an Alpha!"

I couldn't defend myself against his accusation because it was true, and everyone knew it. I remained silent as Eudorus continued, "Look at that! She deceived her own pack mates. what could we expect with all these half breeds? After all, we all saw what happened to Missi, these mixed breeds are all the same. They're nothing but evil troublemakers who were born to hate. She's a traitor to her own pack and she should return to her own kind: the pets! That's what these half breeds do, they're pure evil. She does not belong with us or this pack!"

My blood ran cold as I realized that I could not even defend myself against his speech, because I had lied to them before, how would they know that I wasn't lying to them again?

I took a step back and hesitated before running away into the woods. As usual, Flippy followed me to assure me that what Eudorus said was wrong, "Mysty, they know that Eudorus is prejudice, they'd never believe him over you. They've seen you fight; they know you have nothing but loyalty to your pack."

"But what if Eudorus won't allow me to fight anymore?"

"That would never happen; Luka needs you to lead the army. Eudorus wouldn't risk it."

I decided to believe him, but I still had my doubts, Flippy interrupted those doubts by telling me that Eudorus had sent Thorn to get Luka for more reinforcements since Eudorus refused to admit defeat over the humans.

I wanted to return to Thistle and Eudorus, but I didn't want to expose us to the humans, so I decided to wait until tomorrow when Luka and his reinforcements would arrive.

MONDAY JULY 13, 2020

LUKA WAS WAITING with his reinforcements for me and Flippy. Eudorus did not hesitate to belittle me in front of my own brother, "Glad you could show your sorry mug, mutt." he sneered at me.

I coolly shot back, "Is that any way to talk to your Alpha?"

Eurdorus snarled at me, but before he could fire an insult back, the first gun shot went off and we realized that the humans had followed us and found us.

We fought for hours trying to defeat the humans, I was getting tired, but I perked right back up when I couldn't find Flippy. I stopped fighting and searched for him, but I found Coraltin instead. He was mortally wounded, but I tried to save him, and I failed. When I finally accepted Coraltin's death, I continued the search for Flippy.

I found Flippy a few minutes later, his illness had kicked in and he could barely keep fighting. I instinctively called for a retreat knowing that we could not win this battle; there were just too many humans.

Five humans heard my call and started after me. I yipped before I grabbed Flippy and ran away from the advancing humans. The humans were still on our tails even after we left the battle field far behind. I decided to use evasive maneuvers and lose them in the woods on the mountains again.

After running for almost an hour, I finally managed to outrun the humans and I had lost them. I stopped suddenly and dropped Flippy while I panted heavily.

As I looked around however, I suddenly realized that we were lost, and Flippy was getting sicker.

THURSDAY JULY 16, 2020

I FINALLY CAME to the conclusion that I can't heal Flippy, Athena taught me well, but she had failed to teach me everything before her murder.

I had tried to find the way back by scenting my steps, but the rain from that day of the battle had washed the scent away, as well as destroyed much of the vegetation. It rained every day and night, it never stopped.

I prayed that God would send someone to help us, but it had been three days, and Flippy couldn't afford to wait.

FRIDAY JULY 24, 2020

DESPITE BEING IN the thick forest mountains food had been shockingly scarce, almost nonexistent. Yesterday God answered my prayers. The other night I received a dream from Athena. She told me that Duchess finally discovered her gift: tracking. She notified Sherry and Carry of our location.

"That's great!" I realized that we would be saved, but Athena halted my celebration.

"Mysty, something has been troubling you lately and it's effecting your performance in battle."

"It's Rambo. The last thing he said to me, I don't know why it's affected me so much."

"You should ask him."

"I can't! I can't leave my pack, this is a war!"

"You have to, or next time, you may not be so fortunate." Athena's voice was firm and left no room for debate.

I woke up and looked at Flippy for a moment longer until I rose off the ground. I padded silently away from

Flippy. I knew Sherry and Carry were very close by and Flippy would be fine without me, but I didn't want to leave him.

I felt my eyes getting watery and I silenced a sob before running to the west for the coast. I had to find Rambo, I couldn't return if I didn't find him.

SUNDAY AUGUST 16, 2020

IT WAS HARD to find Rambo on the coast, but I did, and I was quickly turned away.

I was walking on the beach when I heard the yips of pups playing in the near distance. I continued up the coast and saw the pups and Rambo. The pups heard my approach and greeted me eagerly while Rambo hung back.

After greeting the pups I walked up to Rambo. "Pups go play further down the beach while I talk to Mysty."

The pups obeyed and left me and Rambo. Rambo started the conversation first, "I'm still not fighting."

"I'm not asking you to."

"Then why did you come here?"

"The last thing you said to me, about my father dying and the possibility of the rest of us dying. It affected me somehow."

"No it didn't."

"What?" I was puzzled by Rambo's insistence.

"If it affected you, you would have left. You're only

here because you've hit a cross road."

"Yes... lately I've been failing both in battles and healing."

"Because you need to choose. You can't live with a paw on two paths; you'll never get anywhere."

"Can I stay? Here?"

Rambo looked at me uncomfortably before saying, "No, Mysty. You're my best friend, but you represent a part of my life that I can't go back to. I've made my choice. I've chosen a path separate from yours, and you can't follow me. Our paths won't intersect and they head in two different directions. Follow your path, I'm following mine."

I couldn't believe that Rambo could turn me away so coldly. I didn't meet his gaze, I just left. I never said good bye to the pups or to Rambo, I just trotted off into the distance. I said I wouldn't return to the pack until I could serve my pack to my fullest. Now that I knew what the problem was, all that was left was to choose, could I serve my pack better as a fighter or a healer?

MONDAY AUGUST 31, 2020

I HAD SUCH a hard time choosing and I'm not sure why it was so hard for me to choose in the first place. After some quiet time however, I know who I am.

A few days ago I had a dream that I was back in the forest where my pack originally lived and I was not alone, my mother, my father, my late brothers, Slash, Athena, and even Auburn, Cherry, the whole deceased pack; they were all there. They urged me to return to my pack.

"I can't," I told them, "I don't know which path to take."

The pack stared at me silently for a moment, before they all walked up to me and said in unison, "Yes you do Mysty, you always did."

I realized the path that I was supposed to take instantly, and I looked at Athena for approval. Athena looked back at me and nodded her head in acceptance.

When I woke up I knew I could finally go home as a warrior. I was almost there, just a few more days.

THURSDAY SEPTEMBER 3, 2020

I FINALLY RETURNED, but I wished it hadn't took so long for me to come back.

I returned to my pack late in the afternoon. Luka seemed pleased to have me back, and appeared warm in his greeting and announcing my return to the pack, but then I was quickly shot down from my position.

Since I've been gone, Luka fell in love with Tabitha and they officially became mates a few days after my disappearance, meaning that I was no longer the Alpha Female, but I also was not the army's leader either; Flippy was given the position. Then Sherry told me that Duchess had become her apprentice instead of mine. I knew that Duchess would never have been a great warrior, but I was stunned and hurt upon realizing that my best friend had stolen my apprentice.

Now I am just another warrior in the army. The only good news I received was when Flippy reported that

Eudorus had been killed in the last battle I had been in, which was also the last battle we have had so far because the humans have been reorganizing since the death of their general.

MONDAY SEPTEMBER 7, 2020

I RARELY INTERACTED with anyone in the pack except for Flippy and, reluctantly, Sherry. I stayed in my room all day and only came out late at night when everyone else was sleeping. Sherry had suggested we start patrolling the moors to get me out of the city and lift my spirits.

On that night, I wished we had just stayed in the city.

It all began when Sherry and I were going on our usual late night patrols. I had decided to forgive her, but I had yet to even face Duchess. As we were walking closer to where the road was I heard humans. Sherry heard them too and we snuck up on them behind the bushes; there were four humans and Missi was there too.

"I think we should go back for more wolves." I whispered.

"No, we can take them!" Sherry assured me, "Besides they might not still be here by then."

I wanted to argue, but I knew we didn't have the time

to, so instead I finally agreed with her, "Fine, when I give the signal we attack, whatever you do don't let Missi out of your sight."

Sherry nodded at me and I raised my tail to signal a halt. After we pinpointed them, I waved my tail to the right to signal our attack.

We jumped on them and attacked them like rabid wolves. The humans tried to fight back while Missi kept her distance and just watched us fight. We had already killed two of the humans before Missi got involved and attacked Sherry. I fought with the two other humans while Sherry took on Missi.

Missi suddenly yipped for no apparent reason, and the two humans automatically ran off towards the road which was hidden by shrubs, but only a yard away. Missi too took off and I then realized that Missi had sent a signal to the humans.

Sherry chased after them and it was then that I realized that Sherry was unaware of the fact that there was a road behind those bushes.

I tore after her hoping to stop her, but she had run onto the road just as a large truck had appeared only two feet away from her. It was going so fast it was little more than a blur. I heard a loud smack followed by a hollow thud. I searched the road with my eyes until I finally saw Sherry's bloody body.

I ran onto the road and over to her side. Her eyes were

open in a lifeless expression, blood pooled around her, it drained out of her mouth, her nose, her ears, some impact wounds on her body, and a large crack on her head. I didn't want to believe it, but I knew she was dead.

"Oh God. I told you we should have gone back!" I wailed as I realized I had been responsible for my best friend's death. I howled and whimpered as I cried over her lifeless body. So still and silent. I heard a twig snap on the other side of the road and looked up to see Missi staring at us. There was a malicious spark in her eyes and she grinned with sick satisfaction upon seeing Sherry's dead body.

I would have attacked her, but I knew she would have expected me to, and probably had a plan for that very event. Instead I grabbed Sherry's scruff and dragged her off the road and back into the city.

TUESDAY SEPTEMBER 8, 2020

FLIPPY TOLD LUKA that he and Sherry had been out patrolling so as to spare me any further trouble with Luka. It worked, Luka believed him, and Flippy went unpunished. A mercy I doubt I would have also received.

At Sherry's mourning, I noticed that Duchess was grieving, but Carry was emotionless. I confronted Carry about this and asked how she could possibly be so unaffected by the death of her last surviving family member?

Carry simply shrugged and stated, "I learned long ago that during war, and even before and after war, family members leave. I lost my parents who never even loved us, my little sister who was never strong enough to survive anyway, and now my elder sister who cared too much for her own good. In war you have to be cold to survive. It's called adapting."

"I've survived this long, and I'm nothing like you."

"You survived this long; who's to say tomorrow won't be your day? Only I can answer that. But I'll never tell you." she just had to remind me about her creepy psychic gift.

I knew that Carry was right however, any moment could be my last. For that very reason, I have decided to carry my diary with me where ever I go so I can write down my final moments for my loved ones and leave them with messages of reassurance.

SATURDAY SEPTEMBER 12, 2020

WE FOUGHT AGAIN and lost today, but what was truly lost was me.

We were prepared to go to battle as usual, but Hunter, the human army's leader, made a surprise appearance.

Hunter, Luka, and the other animal leaders met in between the armies to discuss something. I strained my ears to pick up their conversation, I could just make out what Hunter was saying,"... and I know you animals aren't gamblers, but I think it makes the fights more interesting. I bet my best warrior that my army will win this battle."

The animal leaders looked at each other nervously, except for Luka who instantly accepted Hunter's challenge, "And I bet my best warrior that we will."

Hunter looked past Luka and stared at me, "I hear that you're best fighter is your own sister, trained by the famous Achilles himself. This does add interest."

My stomach dropped and Flippy cringed once he realized Luka had placed my freedom on the line in a gamble with the humans. I pushed my unease aside hoping to win the battle, but we lost. The humans had dipped their arrows in some sort of paralyzing poison which made it too difficult to fight back; many of my fellow warriors were completely paralyzed by the time the battle was over. I struggled to keep fighting, but I knew that I was done, and then it was over.

Luka was in disbelief, Carry seemed expressionless, but I thought I caught a flicker of smug satisfaction. Duchess and Flippy were horrified, and I was scared. I wanted to whimper, but I knew that I still had to carry an air of dignity; I did represent my father's proud bloodline after all.

Hunter was quick to claim his victory, "I think now I know why animals don't gamble, it's because they lose." Hunter sneered at Luka before setting his sights on me again, "And now, as the victor of this battle, I shall claim my prize in the form of your own sister." Hunter reached down and yanked me up by the scruff.

Flippy snapped at Hunter, but Hunter just gave Flippy a hard, swift kick to the head and Flippy was silenced since the kick was strong enough to knock him out. Duchess yipped and tried to rush to our defense, but she was held back by Carry.

Once Hunter realized that there was no one left to challenge him, he continued dragging me over behind enemy lines.

MONDAY SEPTEMBER 14, 2020

I'M CONVINCED THAT this place is hell.

When I arrived at the human's base, Missi couldn't decide what to do with me, so Hunter decided to put me in the "races". The races involved a dog being tied to a wagon which held only the fattest humans in the human army. The fat humans then whip their wagon dog so they would run up a hill road coated in Vaseline, the hill was tall and steep, and I had never seen anything like it before. The winning dog would live to race another day; the loser was killed since it would be deemed worthless for losing. The rest of the dogs were brutally beaten for not winning.

The humans used the races to feed their gambling addictions as well as entertainment. Apparently they found pleasure in the suffering of animals, and suffering we were. I looked all around me and I saw the same thing, the dogs from the races all had dull, soulless eyes, their fur was matted by the mud, blood, and Vaseline so much that their fur would have to be shaved off so their coats could grow back. Was that my future?

SATURDAY OCTOBER 4, 2020

I HAVE SURPRISED myself by making it to my one year birthday, a land mark I never thought I'd reach in this hell hole.

The races have taken much out of me. Grooming had become a worthless attempt to maintain my life just a bit.

It's becoming harder to keep up with the other dogs in the races. While I could not guarantee a win for myself, I did make sure I never lost. I still clinged to the hope that my pack would save me.

The humans never fed us. We stole whatever scraps we could find and we licked the stone walls of our cells for water. We were always cold and tired as the humans tried to brake us, I however refused to be broken. I still had some will left and I was going to use it.

The one thing that had prevented me from giving up was the thought of seeing Flippy again. If I could live just long enough to see him again, maybe I could survive this war, or at least die happy. That kept me alive and sane.

The other dogs were lifeless; they were the human's pets. Nothing but mindless slaves, much like the human soldiers. They did what their masters commanded, and died when they were ordered to; when they were considered useless.

Only I knew the truth, they were already dead. They had died long ago; all that remained were their bodies.

FRIDAY OCTOBER 16, 2020

I KNEW THAT I should have been saving my energy for the races, but I needed to see my pack again. So yesterday I bilocated back into the city.

The first one I saw was Duchess but I was too transparent for her to have seen me. I followed her and she lead me to the meeting hall, where Carry, Tabitha, Luka, and Flippy had also gathered. They seemed to be discussing a battle plan, so I stayed in the shadows and listened in.

Luka had started off as soon as Duchess arrived, "I have devised an excellent plan for ending this war. I'm planning an invasion. Flippy, I need you to lead our warriors into the humans' base while Tabitha and a few other warriors surround the entrances. Then I want our invading wolves to ignite everything. This will drive them to the exits where the rest of the animals can dispatch the humans who try to escape."

"What about Mysty? She's still in there." Flippy pointed out.

"It's been over a month now Flippy, she's probably dead. Even if she wasn't don't you think she'd want you to do your duty to the pack even if it meant at the cost of her life?" Luka debated.

"She's your own sister! How could you just condemn her to death?" Flippy was clearly shocked by my brother's callousness.

"Because I know where my loyalties lie. Now you have to choose Flippy, the lives of your pack, or just one life: hers."

Flippy remained silent and Luka knew he had won. Luka turned to Tabitha, "We'll attack next month at midnight, spread the word to the other armies."

Tabitha, Carry, and Duchess both nodded at Luka before leaving, Duchess looked back at Flippy but said nothing as she left with her tail hanging low. Luka followed them, leaving Flippy all alone.

I wanted to comfort him, but I knew that if he realized I was still alive he may jeopardize Luka's plan. There was too much riding on his operation and I was not about to ruin our chances of winning. I casted one last longing glance at Flippy before I returned to my body.

FRIDAY NOVEMBER 13, 2020

THE RACES HAD become too hard for me today and I just couldn't handle it anymore.

I struggled to drag myself up that hill, but I slipped at the last minute and slid all the way down the hill. Once we were at the bottom, the human in my wagon kept whipping me, but I had pulled the wagons for two agonizing months and I just couldn't keep doing it any longer. So I stayed down, knowing it would cost me my life.

After the race, Missi herself dragged me to Hunter's tent. "I always wondered how long you'd last." Hunter greeted me. Missi took her leave and Hunter prepared his trusted hand gun. "I'll be honest, you lasted longer than I expected, but I see that even an Alpha has to stand down. Every day is a war and somebody always has to lose. One day I will be that loser, but not before you." Hunter then turned around to face me, with his gun aimed right at my head.

I wanted to run, but I didn't have the energy, if he had

only carried on with that speech a little longer I would have been able to run, but his finger was already squeezing the trigger.

Before he could shoot me however, something red flashed in front of me and attacked Hunter. I watched in complete shock as the red creature ripped out Hunter's throat, but before Hunter could die, he shot the creature. When the creature fell to the ground, I saw it was Luka.

"Luka! Why did you do that?" I wailed.

"Because you're my little sister. It's an older brother's duty to take care of his little sister."

"But you'll die."

"I know. I failed one little sister and I tried to make it right, but I hadn't realized that you can't change the past. And because of that, I lashed out at you. I have always loved you Mysty, but since I lost everyone who I had ever loved, I became numb. I was suffering and I knew that you were too, but I didn't know how to be there for you. I'm sorry that I couldn't be the big brother that you needed, but I hope that this last act of brotherly love will allow you to forgive me for not being there for you when you needed me most."

"I forgive you Luka." I whimpered.

"You're the Alpha now."

"What about Tabitha?"

"She's not pregnant, she can't produce any heirs, and my bloodline ends with you." Luka managed to reveal before his head dropped and he closed his eyes while re-leasing his last breath.

I wanted to stay with my fallen brother and Alpha, but I knew there was still a war to win.

I left the tent and saw the humans' entire base was up in flames; even some humans were on fire as well. Some humans tried to flee, but they were killed instantly by the animals. The new human general was trying to get his soldiers in order, but that was a quickly failing plan.

In all the chaos, my mind was set on one thing, find-ing and killing Missi. I searched long and hard for the wolf dog who had nearly destroyed me, she wasn't in the humans' base, but I found her outside near the gorge with Flippy.

As I ran up to them I heard Missi tell Flippy, "You're too late pup, I ordered her death myself just before your ambush!" Missi was about to gain the upper paw, but I was faster and I jumped on her. Missi slipped out of my grasp and we began to fight. We were like two tornados fighting for dominance. Missi was stronger than me, but I was swifter than her.

I used my swiftness to dodge her blows knowing that she would grow tired eventually, which she did. When she began to slow down, I noticed that she was exposing her chest, a fatal mistake that I had once made as well. Except this time, it would result in her death. I used my now sharp and long claws to burrow in her chest, stabbing her right in the heart.

After that I tried to break away from her, but she grabbed me and said, "I'm not dying alone!" before she pulled both of us off the gorge and into the river.

The water was freezing and the force knocked the breath out of me. I panicked and flailed in the water trying to stay above the waves and also trying to grab onto anything that could help me pull myself out.

I felt some one grab me by the scruff and I knew instantly it was Flippy again. Flippy pulled me back to shore and I shook myself dry.

"You're alive! I can't believe it." Flippy panted.

"It's because of you." I told him.

"What do you mean?"

"The thought of seeing you again was enough to keep me alive for all those months. I love you Flippy."

Flippy looked surprised, but this faded rapidly and was replaced by his puppyish smile, "And I love you too, I always have. I wanted to tell you sooner, but the moment never seemed right."

"Better late than never." I told him as I nuzzled his face.

SUNDAY NOVEMBER 15, 2020

THE HUMANS HAD admitted defeat, but they swore that our war is not over and they would return again.

The animals accepted their admission of defeat and began to leave the city. I was reluctant to leave behind the city which harbored so many memories, some good, and some bad.

Tabitha mourned the loss of Luka, but didn't mind surrendering her position as Alpha Female to me; the rightful heir. I was surprised to learn that I hadn't lost any warriors in the last battle except for Luka.

I felt alone now that I was the last surviving member of my family, but I had Flippy with me to help ease the loneliness.

As we left the city behind, I could not help but feel a twinge of longing to stay, but I knew that we as animals did not belong in a city. We were wild animals and we belonged in the wild. I was ready to lead my pack, however young I may be no one had more experience than I did, not even Eudorus.

EPILOGUE
THURSDAY DECEMBER 31, 2020

FLIPPY AND I bear the titles of Pack Alphas.

I have almost recovered completely from my months of captivity, my whip marks have healed and the fur has nearly grown back, but I am still very skinny.

I knew that our conflict with the humans was not yet solved and one day we might be back to war, but that would be another time and another diary. For that moment, there was nothing but silence on our opposing end.

Tonight everyone in my pack was fast asleep as we were about to enter a new year, but I remained awake. I felt the need to revisit my old haunts to look back on my first year and reflect how far I've come.

I went back to my mother's alley and my memories came to life before my eyes. I saw two wolf dog pups playing together as their Great Dane mother watched, I saw their wolf father come for the eldest pup, and I saw the mother Dane murdered in cold blood while her daughter avenged her mother's death. I saw the father wolf come for his last daughter.

I followed the wolf and his daughter, to the lair of their pack where the daughter was introduced to her brothers and her future mate.

I followed the pack as their leader took them to the Safe City for the war. There I saw the wolf dog mourn the loss of her father, brothers, and friends.

I kept up with the wolf dog and her friend to the road where she witnessed the death of her best friend. The wolf dog ran into the burned down forest where she found the body of one of her mentors.

I then followed her to her last destination, the ruins of the humans' camp where her brother had sacrificed himself in an attempt to make amends, before she killed her traitorous twin.

It was hard for me to believe that I was that wolf dog. I had done those incredible things, I had lived those moments. I had lost those dear friends and kin. My mother, my father, my brothers, my sister, Athena, Slash, Auburn, Cherry, Sherry, Rambo, Articus and Athicus. They were all gone, but I still had Flippy and Duchess. It took me a while, but I did eventually forgive my little coyote sister for becoming Sherry's apprentice.

I returned to my pack and laid back down beside my mate. "Happy new year Mysty." Flippy whispered to me.

"Happy new year Flippy." I greeted back as I buried

my muzzle in his pelt. It had been a hard year, but it was worth it because I knew that nothing would ever separate me from Flippy ever again.

We were free.

CPSIA information can be obtained at www.ICGtesting.com
Printed in the USA
LVOW07s1502120515

438204LV00001B/14/P

9 781478 739586